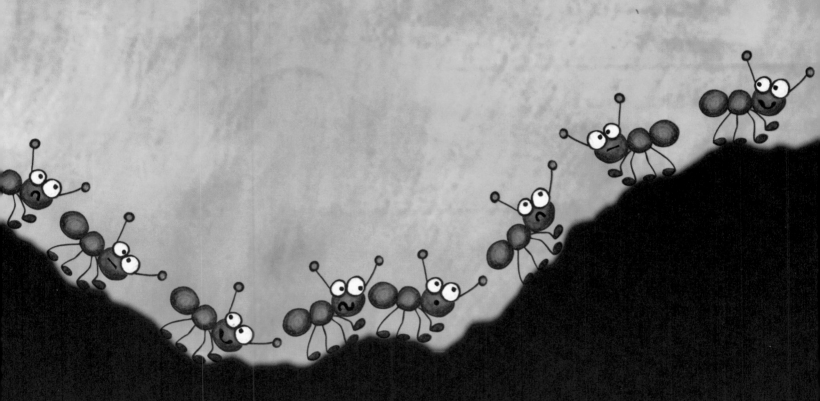

Sue Foley
TYRONE

a Turtle Tale

illustrated by Carrie Kabak

Robert D. Reed Publishers
750 La Playa Street, Suite 647 • San Francisco, CA 94121

Robert D. Reed Publishers

For information regarding permission, please write to:

Dick Foley
6 Longspur Road, Portola Valley, CA 94028

Carrie Kabak
P.O. Box 10188, Kansas City, MO 64171

ISBN 1-885003-88-9

Printed in China

Library of Congress Control Number: 2001090961

"Tyrone can't play!

Tyrone can't play!"

Tyrone wanted to play very much.
"I hate being teased like this,"
he said, blinking away a heavy tear.
Today, he was wearing his
brand new, shiny red glasses.

Mike, the blue turtle, had shown everyone
how to play a special new game called,
TURTLE HIDE and SEEK.
"The one chosen to be IT has to pop their head
inside their shell and shout,

10 9 8 7 6 5 4 3 2 1

No peeking is allowed!" warned Mike.
"The others have to find places to hide
as fast as they can.
The turtle who is IT yells,

here I come, ready or not!"

Tyrone badly wanted to be IT,
but he had one very big problem.
His head would not fit inside his shell.

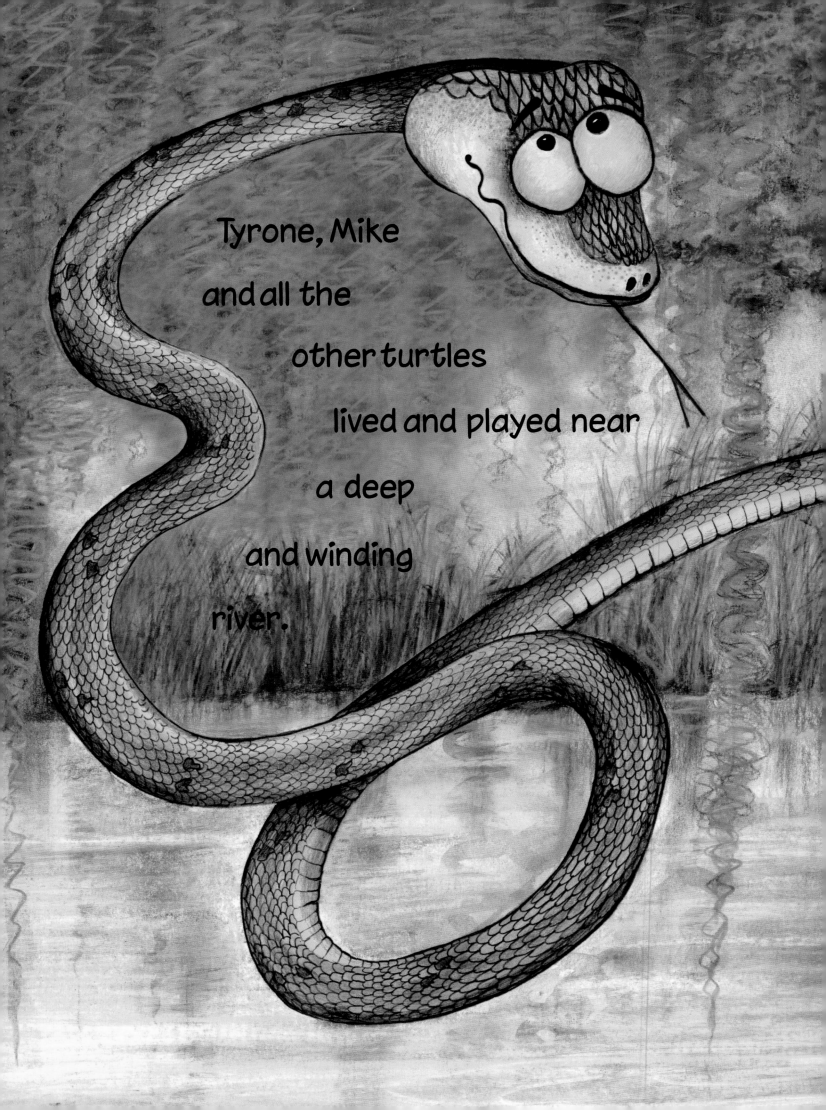

Tyrone, Mike and all the other turtles lived and played near a deep and winding river.

Along the riverbank there were twisted vines, moss covered stumps and hollow logs.

Their home was filled with many

secret passageways and hidden corners that were just perfect for

TURTLE HIDE and SEEK.

Tyrone sighed and made his way
to the edge of the river.
The cool, clear water was like a mirror.
He studied his reflection carefully.

The **brand new, shiny red glasses**
sparkled brightly back at him.
"HUH," he muttered.
"My head is STILL the same size as yesterday."

This made the other turtles laugh at him.
They scampered away to play their new game.

Poor, poor Tyrone was not happy at all.
He just sat there on the soft grass,
all alone, wondering what to do.

Tyrone felt very sad and gloomy.

He decided to visit his river friends.
Maybe they could help solve
this very big problem.

Freddie was a happy, funny frog.
He was lazily sunning himself on a rock.
"Hey Freddie!
Why won't my head go inside my shell any more?"
The frog pondered for a while and suggested,

"Try hopping UP and DOWN and SIDEWAYS

like frogs do and see what happens."

Tyrone H O P P E D UP and DOWN

and *SIDEWAYS* with Freddie.

His head would not pop down inside his shell, no matter how hard he jumped and bounced about.

"STOP !" croaked the frog.
"I just saw Alvin floating by, I bet he can help."

Alvin was a wise alligator.

He took daily trips swimming smoothly
up and down the river.
The cool, moving water helped him slither
along the surface like a floating log.

"Alvin, why won't my head go
inside my shell any more?" asked Tyrone.

The alligator watched the turtle
with his yellow eyes.

The alligator yawned

WIDELY

and grinned.

"Wet your head in the river,
then it will slide back inside your shell."

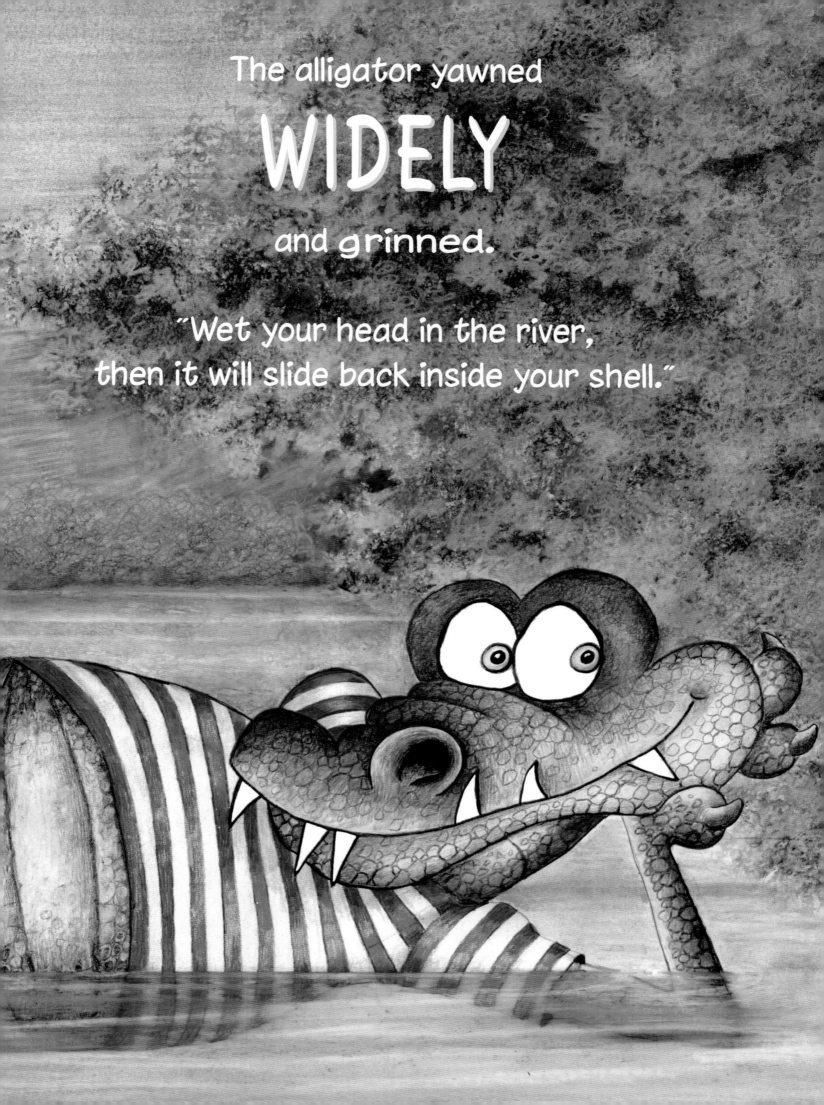

Tyrone chose a spot along the riverbank that was not **too** close to Alvin.

He dipped his head deep into the water.

He tried to slide his head
inside his purple shell.

"OUCH!" grumbled Tyrone.
"My head got stuck half way!"

With his new glasses all spotted and speckled
with droplets of water,
Tyrone meandered along the riverbank.
He would never be IT.

From the top of a grassy mound,
he spied his friend Hildi, a hippopotamus.

Snorting loudly, she surfaced.

"Why are you so sad, Ty?" she boomed.

Tyrone trotted down towards the river's edge.

"I can't play
TURTLE HIDE and SEEK
because we have to pop
our heads inside our shells.
I can't do that any more and I don't know why
and I'll never, ever be IT!"

"You need exercise," Hildi decided.
"Swim and twirl about underwater like me.
You'll soon feel flexible enough to POP
your head inside your shell."

Hildi fluttered her long eyelashes.

The water

gurgled

and bubbled

in his ears

as Tyrone

sank deeply

underwater.

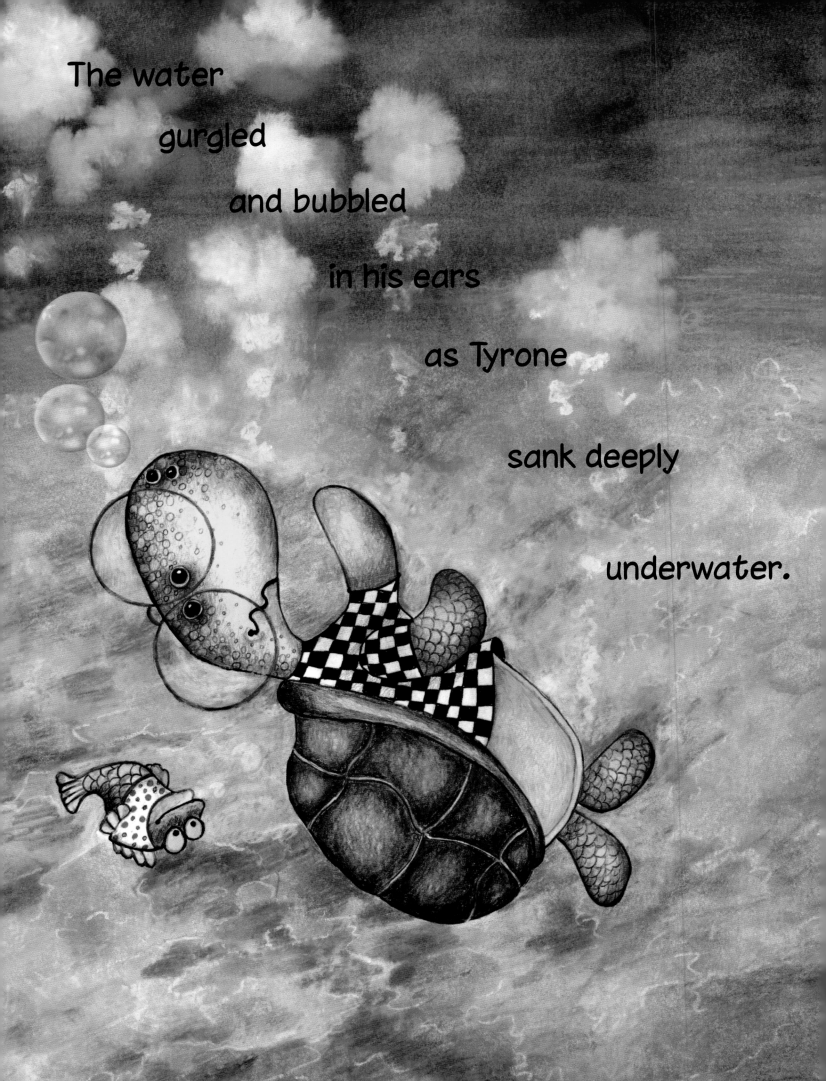

Tyrone swam and twirled and twisted
and tried to pull his head inside his shell.

It was no good. It was no use.
The turtle would have to forget about
ever playing

TURTLE HIDE and SEEK.

"My head has grown too big," he moaned.

Tyrone could hear happy noises in the distance.
The other turtles were still enjoying
their new game.

Suddenly, there were muffled cries and

a CREEEEK and a CRAAAAAAAAAASH!!

˝HELP, I'm trapped! I'm trapped!! HELP!!˝

Mike had been hiding inside a slippery mud hole,
when something awful had happened.
A tree branch had fallen heavily on top of him.
Mike was stuck and he was

Sinking

deeper
and
deeper
into
the
mud.

Tyrone ran as fast as his stumpy little legs could carry him ...

There was the heavy tree branch,
lying across the mud hole.
But where was Mike?

Grabbing the end of the branch,
Tyrone pulled with all his might.

He pulled and pulled and pulled.

The branch slid away slowly and...

there was Mike, covered in smelly mud
and peppered with dry leaves.

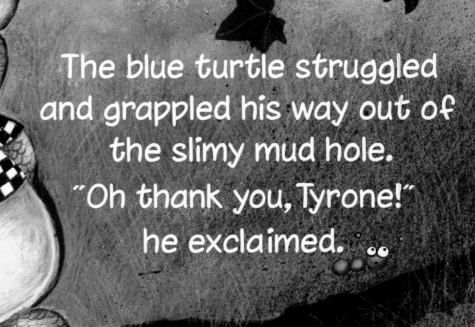

The blue turtle struggled
and grappled his way out of
the slimy mud hole.
"Oh thank you, Tyrone!"
he exclaimed.

Mike waddled off to join his friends again,
leaving a muddy trail behind him.

If Tyrone had not rescued Mike,
what would have happened to him?

Tyrone felt so proud after saving Mike.
"HURRAY for Tyrone! Well done! TY...Ty...Tyrone!"
What were those squawking, screeching sounds?

"Who are you? WHERE are you?" asked the
puzzled turtle.

It was Patrick, the parrot, peering down.
He was swinging from a leafy branch.

Even though Tyrone wore
brand new, shiny red glasses,
he could not see Patrick.

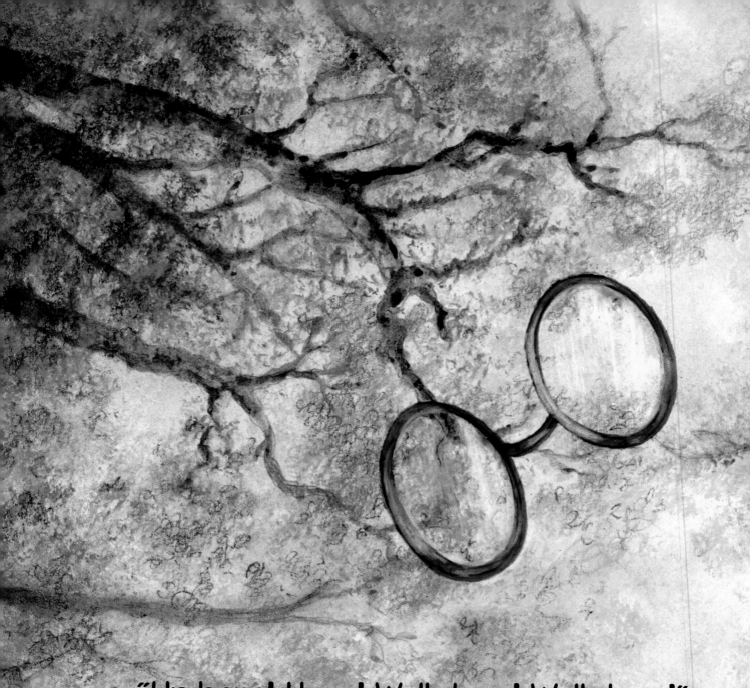

"Up here! Here! Well done! Well done!"
squealed Patrick.

Tyrone clambered up a steep, mossy tree trunk.

He peered upwards at the leaves and the sky,
searching for Patrick's bright parrot feathers.

The sun glinted brightly in the turtle's eyes,
making him squint.

"Ty, Ty, Ty, Tyrone!
Are you alright? Are you alright?"
squeaked Patrick.

The turtle was not sure if he was alright.

He did not hurt, but everything looked BLACK.

It was so dark, he wondered if the sun had fallen out of the sky.

Patrick suddenly SCREECHED.
"Your head's inside your shell!

TYRONE! YOUR HEAD'S INSIDE!

INSIDE YOUR SHELL!"

Tyrone bobbed his head in and out of his shell
GLEEFULLY!
Trouble was, the world outside his shell
seemed very BLURRY.

Where were Tyrone's
brand new, shiny red glasses?

Suddenly, a HUGE,

WIDE GRIN

appeared on the turtle's face.
"Ohhhhh" and "ahhhhh!"
he beamed.

Tyrone rushed off to find his friends.

There they were, laughing and giggling, about to start a new game of

TURTLE HIDE and SEEK.

"Look at me!" yelled Tyrone, happily.
"I can play with you now!"

He took off his
brand new, shiny red glasses
and pulled his head inside his shell.

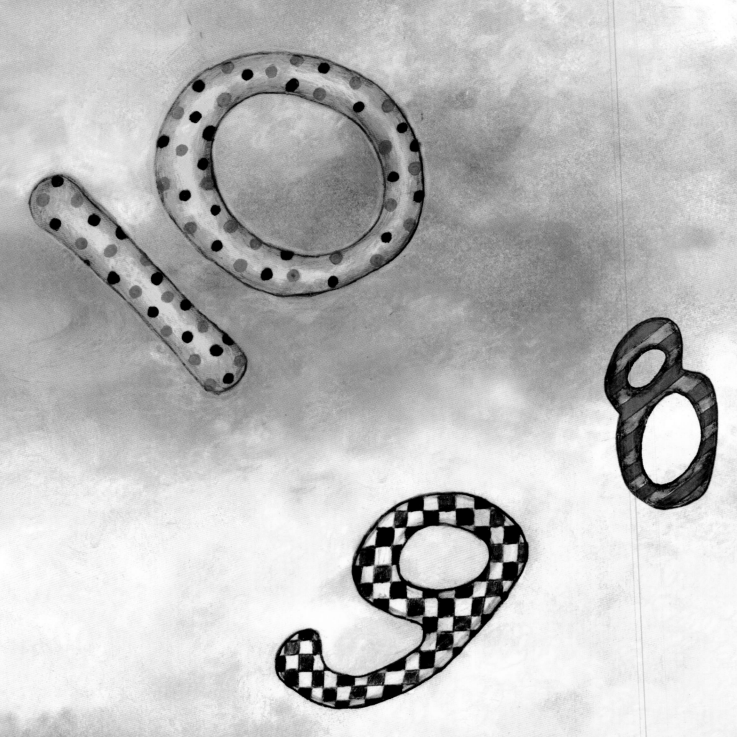

Everyone clapped and cheered for Tyrone!!
"I'll be IT now!" Tyrone was such a happy turtle.

Taking off his
brand new, shiny red glasses
once more, he pulled his head inside his shell
with a `POP.´

(He did not peek.)

5 4
6   3
      2
7   1

Here I come, ready or not!

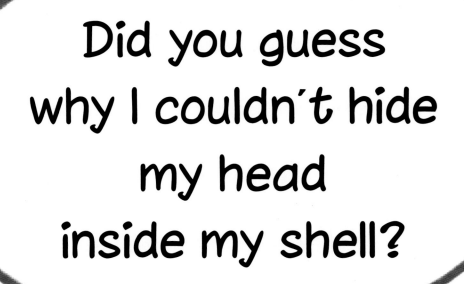

Sue Foley

The author was baptised Dorothy Anne by her parents, but re-baptised "Susie-Q" by her then six year old brother Richard, naming her after his best friend's sister. Suzie Q became Suzie, which evolved to Sue, and by which she was known from that time on. Sue suffered from astigmatism and wore glasses at age two, which perhaps served as the impetus for this tale of overcoming adversity.

Sue graduated from Bowling Green University with a Bachelor's degree in Education, and from San Jose State with a Master's degree in Library Science. She was an elementary school teacher for 20 years, an accomplished artist, and an active member of her community, serving as the Vice President of the California Grand Jurors Association.

Sue died from breast cancer at age 45, after a courageous two-year battle. Prior to her death in 1990, she lived in Watsonville, California, and was the Media Center Director for Amesti School, a grade school that primarily serves children of migrant farm workers.

"Tyrone, a Turtle Tale" was completed shortly before her death and is being published posthumously by her brother. The proceeds will be donated for breast cancer research at the University of California at San Francisco's Comprehensive Cancer Center. (www.cc.ucsf.edu).

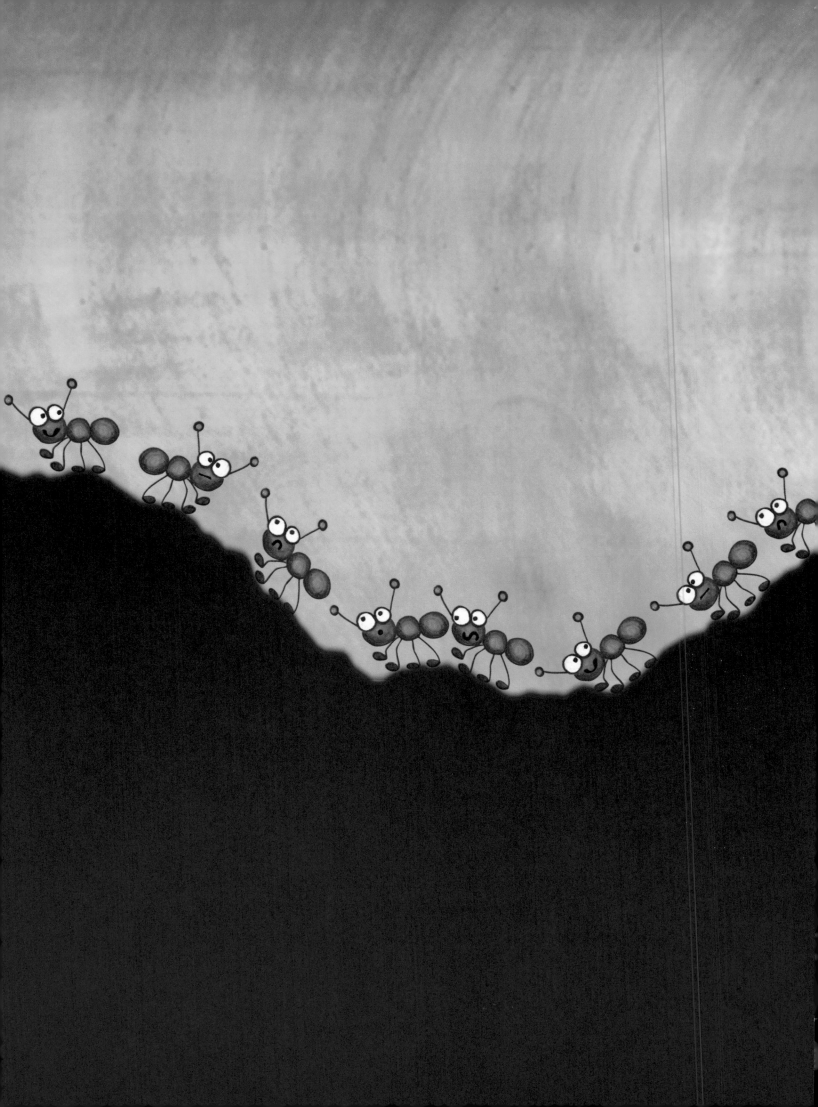